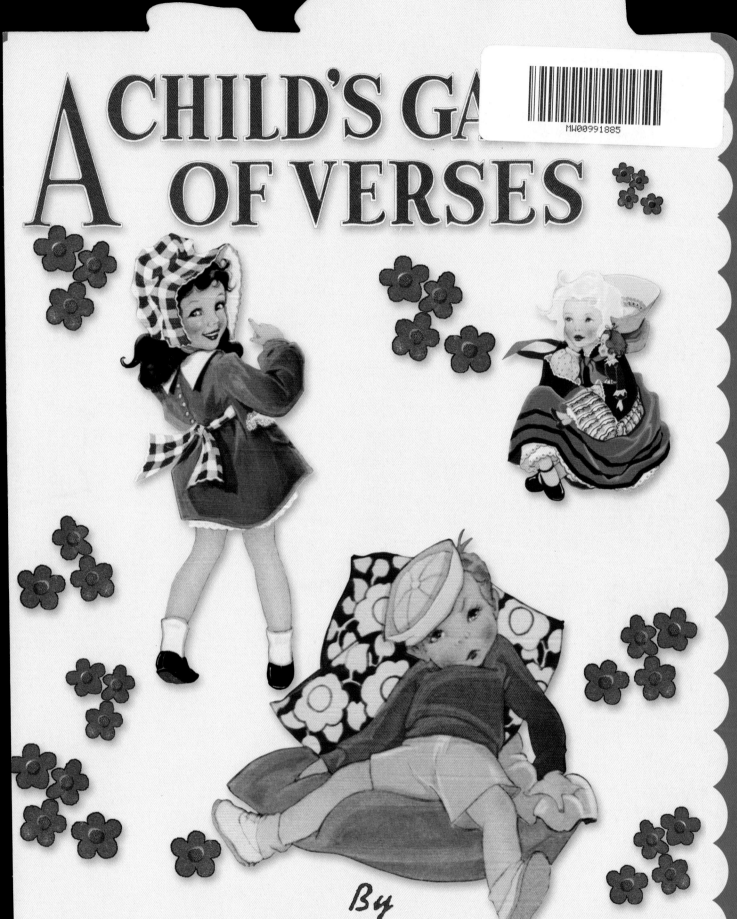

A CHILD'S GARDEN OF VERSES

By
ROBERT LOUIS STEVENSON

Illustrations by
FERN BISEL PEAT

LAUGHING ELEPHANT MMXIII

RAIN

The rain is raining all around,
It falls on field and tree,

It rains on the umbrellas here,
And on the ships at sea.

MY SHIP AND I

O it's I that am the captain of a tidy little ship,
    Of a ship that goes a-sailing on the pond;
And my ship it keeps a-turning all around and all about;
But when I'm a little older, I shall find the secret out
    How to send my vessel sailing on beyond.

For I mean to grow as little as the dolly at the helm,
    And the dolly I intend to come alive;
And with him beside to help me, it's a-sailing I shall go,
It's a-sailing on the water, when the jolly breezes blow
    And the vessel goes a divie-divie-dive.

O it's then you'll see me sailing through the rushes and the reeds,
    And you'll hear the water singing at the prow;
For beside the dolly sailor, I'm to voyage and explore,
To land upon the island where no dolly was before,
    And to fire the penny cannon in the bow.

A GOOD PLAY

We built a ship
    upon the stairs
All made of the back-bedroom chairs,
And filled it full of sofa pillows
To go a-sailing on the billows.

    We took a saw and several nails,
    And water in the nursery pails;
    And Tom said, "Let us also take
    An apple and a slice of cake;"—
    Which was enough for Tom and me
    To go a-sailing on, till tea.

We sailed along for days and days,
And had the very best of plays;
But Tom fell out and hurt his knee,
So there was no one left but me.

WHERE GO THE BOATS?

Dark brown is the river,
    Golden is the sand.
It flows along for ever,
    With trees on either hand.

Green leaves a-floating,
    Castles of the foam,
Boats of mine a-boating—
    Where will all come home?

On goes the river
And out past the mill,
Away down the valley,
Away down the hill.

Away down the river,
    A hundred miles or more,
Other little children
    Shall bring my boats ashore.

THE SWING

How do you like to go up in a swing,
 Up in the air so blue?
Oh, I do think it the pleasantest thing
 Ever a child can do!

Up in the air and over the wall,
 Till I can see so wide,
Rivers and trees and cattle and all
 Over the countryside—

Till I look down on the garden green,
 Down on the roof so brown—
Up in the air I go flying again,
 Up in the air and down!

AUTUMN FIRES

In the other gardens
 And all up the vale,
From the autumn bonfires
 See the smoke trail!

Pleasant summer over
 And all the summer flowers,
The red fire blazes,
 The grey smoke towers.

Sing a song of seasons!
 Something bright in all!
Flowers in the summer,
 Fires in the fall!

THE LAND OF COUNTERPANE

When I was sick and lay a-bed,
I had two pillows at my head,
And all my toys beside me lay
To keep me happy all the day.

And sometimes for an hour or so
I watched my leaden soldiers go,
With different uniforms and drills,
Among the bed-clothes, through the hills;

And sometimes sent my ships in fleets
All up and down among the sheets;
Or brought my trees and houses out,
And planted cities all about.

I was the giant great and still
That sits upon the pillow-hill,
And sees before him, dale and plain,
The pleasant land of counterpane.

SINGING

Of speckled eggs the birdie sings
   And nests among the trees;
The sailor sings of ropes and things
   In ships upon the seas.

The children sing in far Japan,
   The children sing in Spain;
The organ with the organ man
   Is singing in the rain.

THE WIND

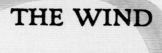

I saw you toss the kites on high
And blow the birds about the sky;
And all around I heard you pass,
Like ladies' skirts across the grass—
　　O wind, a-blowing all day long,
　　O wind, that sings so loud a song!

I saw the different things you did,
But always you yourself you hid.
I felt you push, I heard you call,
I could not see yourself at all—
　　O wind, a-blowing all day long,
　　O wind, that sings so loud a song!

O you that are so strong and cold,
O blower, are you young or old?
Are you a beast of field and tree,
Or just a stronger child than me?
　　O wind, a-blowing all day long,
　　O wind, that sings so loud a song!

TIME TO RISE

A birdie with a yellow bill
Hopped upon the window sill,

Cocked his shining eye and said:
"Ain't you 'shamed, you sleepy-head!"

BED IN SUMMER

In winter I get up at night
And dress by yellow candle-light.
In summer, quite the other way,
I have to go to bed by day.

I have to go to bed and see
The birds still hopping on the tree,
Or hear the grown-up people's feet
Still going past me in the street.

And does it not seem hard to you,
When all the sky is clear and blue,
And I should like so much to play,
To have to go to bed by day?

MARCHING SONG

Bring the comb and play upon it!
　　Marching, here we come!
Willie cocks his highland bonnet,
　　Johnnie beats the drum.

Mary Jane commands the party,
　　Peter leads the rear;
Feet in time, alert and hearty,
　　Each a Grenadier!

All in the most martial manner
　　Marching double-quick;
While the napkin, like a banner,
　　Waves upon the stick!

Here's enough of fame and pillage,
　　Great Commander Jane!
Now that we've been round the village,
　　Let's go home again.

PIRATE STORY

Three of us afloat in the meadow by the swing,
    Three of us aboard in the basket on the lea.
Winds are in the air, they are blowing in the spring,
    And waves are on the meadow like the waves there are at sea.

Where shall we adventure, to-day that we're afloat,
    Wary of the weather and steering by a star?
Shall it be to Africa, a-steering of the boat,
    To Providence, or Babylon, or off to Malabar?

MY SHADOW

I have a little shadow that goes in and out with me,
And what can be the use of him is more than I can see.
He is very, very like me from the heels up to the head;
And I see him jump before me, when I jump into my bed.

The funniest thing about him is the way he likes to grow—
Not at all like proper children, which is always very slow;
For he sometimes shoots up taller like an india-rubber ball,
And he sometimes gets so little that there's none of him at all.

He hasn't got a notion of how children ought to play,
And can only make a fool of me in every sort of way.
He stays so close beside me, he's a coward you can see;
I'd think shame to stick to nursie as that shadow sticks to me!

One morning, very early, before the sun was up,
I rose and found the shining dew on every buttercup;
But my lazy little shadow, like an arrant sleepy-head,
Had stayed at home behind me and was fast asleep in bed.

THE LAMPLIGHTER

My tea is nearly ready and the sun
has left the sky;
It's time to take the window to see Leerie
going by;
For every night at tea-time and before you take your seat,
With lantern and with ladder he comes posting up the stree

For we are very lucky, with a lamp before the door,
And Leerie stops to light it as he lights so many more;
And oh! before you hurry by with ladder and with light,
O Leerie, see a little child and nod to him to-night!

FAREWELL TO THE FARM

The coach is at the door at last;
The eager children, mounting fast
And kissing hands, in chorus sing:
Good-bye, good-bye, to everything!

To house and garden, field and lawn,
The meadow-gates we swang upon,
To pump and stable, tree and swing,
Good-bye, good-bye, to everything!

And fare you well for evermore,
O ladder at the hayloft door,
O hayloft where the cobwebs cling,
Good-bye, good-bye, to everything!

Crack goes the whip, and off we go;
The trees and houses smaller grow;
Last, round the woody turn we swing:
Good-bye, good-bye, to everything!

Laughing
ELEPHANT

COPYRIGHT © 2011, BLUE LANTERN STUDIO

ISBN/EAN: 9781595834294

THIS PRODUCT CONFORMS TO CPSIA 2011

SECOND PRINTING • PRINTED IN CHINA THROUGH COLORCRAFT LTD., HONG KONG • ALL RIGHTS RESERVED
THIS IS A REPRINT OF A BOOK FIRST PUBLISHED BY
THE SAALFIELD PUBLISHING COMPANY

LAUGHING ELEPHANT
3645 INTERLAKE AVENUE NORTH SEATTLE, WA 98103

LAUGHINGELEPHANT.COM